Mini Mysteries 2

20 more Tricky Tales to Untangle

By Rick Walton

Illustrated by Lauren Scheuer

Published by American Girl Publishing

Questions or comments? Call 1-800-845-0005, visit our Web site at **americangirl.com**, or write to Customer Service, American Girl, 8400 Fairway Place, Middleton, WI 53562-0497.

Printed in China

13 14 15 16 17 18 LEO 16 15 14 13 12 11

Editorial Development: Trula Magruder

Art Direction & Design: Chris Lorette David

Production: Mindy Rappe, Kendra Schluter, Jeannette Bailey, Judith Lary

Illustrations: Lauren Scheuer

Dear Reader,

Do you like to crack cases? Uncover clues? Identify suspects? Look inside! You'll find another year of mini mysteries waiting for a super sleuth like you.

Read the story and then try to figure out the whodunit along with Marie and her pals. But beware of red herrings—those false leads that can send you in the wrong direction.

Once you think you've found a solution, open the "case closed" folder in back to check your answer.

Happy sleuthing!

Your friends at American Girl

Contents

BROOKE

FAith

Absent Present

Marie misses the gift presentation at the party. Will her problem-solving skills help her out?

"What did you get Faith?" Marie asked as she walked to Faith's birthday party with Noelle.

"This," said Noelle. She held up a rectangular present, brightly wrapped, ribboned, and bowed.

"I know that," said Marie. "But what's in it?"

Noelle smiled. "You'll find out along with everyone else. What did you get her?"

Marie smiled and held out her gift bag, brimming with tissue paper. "This."

When the girls reached Faith's house, Marie rang the doorbell. Faith answered. "You're the first ones here," she said. She took their presents and put them on a small table just inside the door.

The doorbell rang again. It was Hope. "Didn't start the party without me, did you?" She pulled a tiny wrapped gift from her pocket and handed it to Faith.

Sage and Hailey arrived together. "Hope you haven't already seen this," Sage said as she handed Faith her gift.

"I haven't," said Hope. Sage made a face at her.

Everyone had arrived, so Faith ushered all the girls into the living room, and the party began.

The girls played games.

They had a treasure hunt.

They ate pizza.

They sang "Happy Birthday."

They sang "Happy Birthday" again, only louder and more off-key.

And they had cake and ice cream.

Then it was time for the presents. Marie helped Faith carry in the presents from the small table. They put the gifts on the floor, and all the girls sat around them.

Faith picked Marie's to open first. She pulled out the tissue and looked inside the bag. Then she gave Marie a puzzled look.

Marie looked in the bag. It was empty! "Oh, no!" she said. "I was so worried about the tissue paper looking great that I forgot to put the present in the bag! I'll run home and get it. Keep opening presents, and I'll be right back."

In ten minutes, Marie was back.

She rang the bell. Faith yelled, "Come in!"

Marie found Faith sitting in the living room. In front of her were her opened presents—a DVD, a teddy bear, a bracelet, and a puzzle book.

She handed Faith her gift bag. Faith pulled out a gel pen set. As she oohed and aahed, Marie figured out who had given each present.

Absent Present

Can you?

Here's a gift—the answer is on page 81.

A Stormy Shortcut

Everyone's dressed up and the clock's ticking.
Will Brooke make it in time?

"Here's Hope!" said Noelle as she let her friend in from the pouring summer rainstorm.

"Someone get me a towel," said Hope. "Good thing my mom had a raincoat I could borrow."

"Now we're waiting for Brooke," said Marie. She looked at her watch.

The girls were ready to take off as soon as Brooke arrived. They'd been invited to help out at an art exhibit at a gallery that one of Mrs. Dee's friends owned. They'd take coats, hand out programs and refreshments, clean up—whatever needed to be done. It was going to be a fancy event, and the girls were dressed in their best.

As the minutes ticked away, the girls started getting nervous. Would they get there on time?

"Any sign of Brooke yet?" Mrs. Dee asked. Noelle's mom would be driving the girls to the event.

"Not yet. Sorry, Mom," said Noelle.

Mrs. Dee sighed and turned back toward the kitchen for her coffee.

"She's really late," said Faith. "I hope she's O.K."

And then, finally, came a knock. "Brooke!" the girls shouted in unison.

Noelle opened the door, and in came Brooke. She took off her raincoat and the girls gasped.

"Where did you get that dress?" asked Faith. "It's gorgeous! And those shoes!"

Brooke's red dress sparkled, as did her shiny red shoes. They flickered with each step Brooke took.

"My grandmother gave them to me for an early birthday present," said Brooke.

"How did you get here?" asked Noelle. "Did your grandma drive you?"

"No," said Brooke. "That's why I'm late. I walked. I thought I'd take a shortcut. Big mistake! I had to cut through the Jensens' yard, walk over the Thomsons' deck, and climb through that hole in your back fence, Noelle."

"Dad was going to fix that, but the rain got in the way."

"And then I had to walk across your soggy backyard. When are you getting grass, Noelle?"

"Dad's hoping to lay a lawn next week. I promised to help. The boys keep tracking dirt in and Mom's getting annoyed, so she told Dad he has to lay the grass soon or she's going to hire someone to do it."

"Well, it would've made my trip easier."

Marie laughed. "Your stories are better, Brooke, but you still need to work on them. This one had a glaring error."

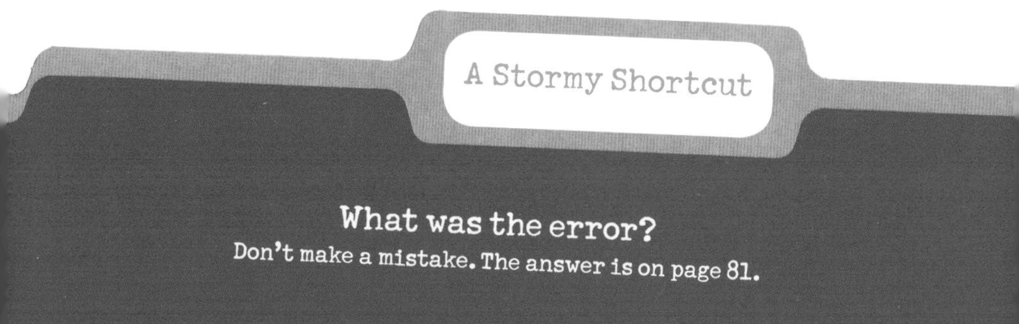

The Long, Dark Hall

Someone's following Marie and Noelle down a dark hallway. Will the girls figure out who?

"I wish I could play like that," said Noelle.

"You could if you practiced as much as I do," Hailey replied.

Hailey had amazed Marie and Noelle at the piano recital—and everyone else who was packed into the school's music room.

After the recital, Marie and Noelle had stayed and talked with Hope, Sage, Faith, Matt, and Nate and then, after the crowd had disappeared, with Hailey.

"Girls, are you coming?" It was Noelle's dad, poking his head through one of the music room doorways, the doorway that led outside to the parking lot.

"My family's waiting for me, too," said Hailey. She hugged Noelle and Marie, waved to Matt and Nate, who were speaking with the janitor, and headed out.

"We'll be right there, Dad," said Noelle, "but I have to run and get my homework. I left it in our classroom. Come with me, Marie?"

The girls raced through the other music room doorway and out into the long hall that ran down the center of the school.

Then they stopped.

"It's dark," said Marie. "Can you even see where you're going?"

"Wait just a minute and our eyes will get used to it."

Before long the girls saw the shape of the hall. They walked slowly across the hard tiled floor.

"I don't think I like this," said Noelle. "What if someone's hiding in a doorway?"

"We can go back," said Marie.

"No, my homework's due tomorrow."

They almost tiptoed down the hallway until their eyes grew more accustomed to the dark and they saw more shapes.

"What's that?" asked Noelle, pointing to a shadow.

"A drinking fountain?"

"Oh yeah," said Noelle. "And that?"

"A . . . I don't know."

"I don't want to find out!" said Noelle. She began to run.

And that's when they heard the footsteps. Behind them.

"Someone's following us!" shouted Noelle. The girls ran even faster.

Then the footsteps ran faster.

"It's probably Matt or Nate," said Noelle, "trying to scare us. But I'm not turning to look."

Noelle grabbed Marie's arm and jerked her into a side hallway. They stopped and held perfectly still.

The footsteps stopped, too.

"Do you think we lost them?" whispered Noelle.

"I don't know," said Marie. "Maybe they're just waiting for us. Look and see if they're still there."

"No, you look," said Noelle.

Marie slowly poked her head around the corner and scanned the main hall.

She pulled her head back. "There's no one there—no one that I can see, anyway."

"Maybe it's a ghost!"

"Ghosts don't make footsteps," said Marie.

"How do you know? Have you ever seen a ghost? It's probably just the janitor," Noelle added.

"Whoever's been chasing us, I think they're gone," said Marie. She dragged Noelle out into the hall, and they started walking toward their classroom. And then they ran.

And there were the footsteps again!

"Stop!" whispered Marie. She grabbed Noelle.

They stopped.

The footsteps stopped.

"We have to go!" said Noelle. "They're still behind us!"

Marie smiled. "I don't think so. Now I know whose footsteps were following us!" she said.

What had Marie figured out?

For a step in the right direction, turn to page 81.

Poor Little Puppy

Fluffball is missing! But who could have taken the dog right out from under the girls' noses?

"Fluffball's so cute!" said Sage.

"Oh, I want to see her," whined Hope.

"Me, too," said Noelle. "I love puppies. But what happens if someone claims her?"

"It's been a month since we found her," said Sage. "Animal Control says she's ours now. They think someone just abandoned her."

"Poor thing!" said Noelle.

"How could anyone abandon a puppy like that?" asked Marie. "She's adorable!"

"I don't know," said Sage. "She must have been so frightened, all alone in the streets."

"So," said Hope, "can we see her again?"

"How about tonight?" asked Sage. "I'll call Mom and see if we can have a sleepover. Let's start at 6:30."

At 6:30, Sage opened the door for her friends. "You got here just in time," she said. "We're about to have a storm."

As though on cue, the thunder cracked. Immediately, from behind Sage came a loud, sharp barking. The barking

continued ferociously as Sage moved aside, revealing a poodle puppy.

"She always barks at thunder," shouted Sage over the roar. The girls laughed, adding to the noise.

Finally the racket stopped. "I don't know who's louder, the thunder or the dog," said Marie.

"She is loud," said Sage. "Poor thing. I hope she gets over it."

Hope reached down to pick up Fluffball, but the puppy scurried away and hid behind Sage's legs.

"She's a very clingy dog," said Sage. "She follows me everywhere. But once she gets used to you, I think she'll let you pet her."

The girls watched Fluffball quietly. Then Sage said, "I'm hungry. Let's get something to eat."

"Sounds good to me," said Hope.

The girls headed to the kitchen with Fluffball close at Sage's heels.

"How about grilled cheese?" asked Sage.

"I love grilled-cheese sandwiches," said Marie.

Sage pulled out a frying pan, bread, butter, and cheese, and the girls went to work. Fluffball begged at their feet until Sage gave her a slice of cheese. The puppy gobbled down the cheese, and then sniffed around the kitchen for more.

"At least she's not hanging around your feet," said Marie.

"Yeah," said Sage. "That's a good sign. Maybe she's feeling more comfortable. She likes to explore, but she always stays in the same room with me."

Sage flipped the sandwich in the pan. The toasted side was a perfect golden brown.

"Almost ready," said Sage. "The only thing we need now is root beer. There's some in the garage. I'll go out and get it."

By the time Sage returned with the soda, the other girls had the sandwiches on the table. "Smells good," said Sage.

The sandwich platter was almost empty when thunder clapped again. The girls covered their ears, expecting to hear Fluffball's barking.

But all they heard was silence.

They looked around. "Where's Fluffball?" asked Noelle. "I don't hear her."

Sage jumped up and poked around the kitchen. With

the other girls' help, she searched under chairs and in boxes, drawers, and cabinets. She even opened up the refrigerator.

No Fluffball.

"I'm worried," said Sage. "Where is she?"

"Let's spread out and look for her," said Marie.

The girls crawled under beds, peeked behind sofas and chairs, ducked under tables, and poked in closets. They searched every room in the house.

No Fluffball.

"She's gotten out and run away!" said Hope.

"She wouldn't do that," said Sage. "Someone's grabbed her! She's so small that anyone could snatch her in a second."

"Let's think about this," said Noelle. "When was the last time we saw Fluffball?"

Then Marie smiled. "I think I know where she is!"

And Marie led the girls right to Fluffball.

Poor Little Puppy

Where was the frightened little puppy?

Doggone it! You'll need to turn to page 81 to find out.

Give Me a Ring

Marie and Noelle find treasure up in a tree. But is it really finders keepers?

"So, are we going roller-skating or not?" asked Noelle. "It's getting late."

The girls had just walked home from school and now stood outside Marie's house.

"Sure," said Marie. "I don't have any homework tonight. And it looks like the weather will be—" Marie looked up to the sky. "What's that?"

"What?" asked Noelle.

Marie pointed toward the top of the tree next to the road in front of Noelle's house. "That blue thing there, hanging from that top tree limb."

Noelle looked.

"Probably just something one of my brothers threw up there."

Marie squinted. "There's a string tied to it, and something's tied to the end of the string. Something gold."

"Gold?" said Noelle. "I like gold. Maybe our tree's sprouting nuggets. Or a squirrel tried to hide a golden acorn. Or a raven found a rich lady's brooch. We're going to be rich!" She squinted. "I'm going to climb up and see what it is."

Noelle sprinted to the tree, grabbed a low branch, and pulled herself up onto it.

"Be careful," said Marie.

"I've been climbing this tree since I was three," said Noelle. "And I haven't fallen yet."

"Yeah, but it was shorter then."

Noelle climbed, branch to branch, up the tree, until she reached the branch with the blue thing hanging on it. She lay down on the branch and inched her way out.

"It's a popped balloon!" Noelle shouted down to Marie. She pulled up the string. "And the gold thing is a ring! With diamonds on it!"

"So *you* found my ring!" said a voice behind Marie.

Marie turned. A girl a couple of years older stood there, hand above her eyes, squinting into the tree.

"How do we know it's your ring?" asked Marie.

"Well," said the girl, "how many rings tied to balloons do you think there are around here?"

By now Noelle had climbed down with the balloon and the ring.

"She says the ring's hers," said Marie.

"How did it get in the tree?" asked Noelle.

"I blew up a balloon for my baby brother to play with," said the girl. "I didn't want it to float away, so I tied my ring to it to keep it on the ground. But the ring wasn't heavy enough, so the balloon floated away. I've been watching it soar around the block. I lost it for a little while, but then you found it for me. Now, if you'll just give it to me, I need to get home."

"I don't think so," said Marie. "That ring might fly, but your story sure doesn't."

What was wrong with the girl's story?

For a ring of truth, turn to page 81.

Nobody's Home

Noelle's friends have disappeared!
Now what should she do?

"Tonight it is," Hilary said to Noelle over the phone.

"It's 2186 Timpview Drive," shouted her twin sister, Margaret, in the background.

Noelle nodded at Marie and said aloud, "2186—I remember. I'm sure I can get us there."

"If we don't answer, just come in," Hilary announced into the receiver. "We'll be in our bedroom working on homework."

Noelle had met Hilary and Margaret at summer camp. She'd visited their house once. This time, Hilary and Margaret had invited Marie, too.

Finding Timpview Drive wasn't hard. It was one of the main roads in Mountain Estates, a new development where all the houses looked the same.

As Noelle's mom drove down the street, the girls watched the numbers. "There's 2096—," Noelle called out, "—2114, 2132." Then Noelle shouted, "Here it is! Right next door to 2150."

Mrs. Dee stopped the car. The girls jumped out, and Noelle marched up to the door and knocked. No answer.

She turned the knob and pushed the door open.

"Uh, Noelle . . ."

"It's O.K., Marie," said Noelle, stepping into the foyer. "They said to just walk in."

"They've redecorated," Noelle shouted to Marie. "It's really nice."

Noelle continued to talk to herself. "And I love the new flowered couch! But the other one was pretty, too. It was pink and green, I think."

Noelle headed down the hall toward the girls' bedroom. "Hilary? Margaret?"

No answer.

Noelle glanced up at all the photos hanging on the walls. They sure had a lot of family members. She had met some of the girls' relatives, but they weren't in any of these family pictures.

Noelle reached the girls' bedroom. She knocked on

their door. Still no answer.

Slowly, Noelle turned the knob and pushed the door open, but the room was empty. No beds, no dressers, no desks, and no girls.

"Marie?" said Noelle quietly, thinking her friend was right with her. Then she turned and shouted, "Marie!"

Where was Marie?

Noelle screamed. Down the hall she raced, past the family photos, by the floral sofa, through the foyer, out the front door, and onto the porch where Marie stood waiting.

"Marie!" shouted Noelle. "I thought you had disappeared along with Hilary and Margaret."

Marie smiled. "I'm right here. And I suspect they're right where they said they'd be, too."

Where were Hilary and Margaret?

Lost? Turn to page 81.

The Neighbor's Garden

The girls volunteer for community service. Will they discover a hidden truth about a neighbor?

"I don't like the look of this place," said Sage.

"It's a little messy," said Hailey, "but that's why we're here—to help Mrs. Duncan clean up her yard."

"Messy?" said Sage. "Look at that garden. Who knows what's hiding under all those weeds."

"We're going to find out," said Marie.

Sage turned to Hailey. "When your mom asked us to help out your elderly neighbor, I was willing, but this place is really creepy."

The girls had arrived at Hailey's this Saturday morning dressed in work clothes and carrying hoes and rakes.

"Mom says Mrs. Duncan just can't get around like she used to," said Hailey. "She tinkers in her yard quite a bit, but she doesn't have the energy to control her weeds. She'll really appreciate everyone's help."

"Well, hello, girls!" said Mrs. Duncan when she met them at her door. "Thank you so much for helping me. These old bones just don't move as well as I'd like them to."

"We're happy to help, Mrs. Duncan," said Hailey.

"Where would you like us to start?"

"Oh, I don't know. There's so much to do. Anyplace you want to work is fine with me. I doubt you can get everything done that needs to be done, but anything you do will be a big help. I'm just happy to have you here."

"Why don't we each just choose a section of the yard and work on it?" said Marie. "I'll take the lawn. Mrs. Duncan, if you'll show me your mower, I'll make this lawn look beautiful."

"And I can trim your bushes," said Noelle.

"And I'll start weeding in your garden," said Hailey. "Sage, how about helping me?"

Mrs. Duncan was happy with the arrangement, and the girls set off to work.

"They all look like weeds to me," said Sage.

"I'll show you which is which," said Hailey. "See these, with the long leaves that look like grass? Pull those out. And the ones with the thorns— pull those out too. That's why we brought these gloves."

Hailey and Sage began weeding. Soon they heard the sound of clippers snapping at branches, and the roar of the lawn mower.

And then, a scream pierced the air.

Noelle dropped the clippers. Marie turned off the mower. They both ran to the garden.

There stood Sage, with a look of horror. She pointed at a mound of dirt. At the head of the mound was a stake. On a plaque on the stake was written "Angelica."

Then she pointed at another mound, another plaque, and the name "Rosemary."

Finally, the girls understood the scream. They all turned to look at a plaque at the head of a partially filled hole in the ground. On it was the name "Sage."

"What does this mean?" asked Noelle. "What do you know about Mrs. Duncan, Hailey?"

"I don't know," said Hailey. "She always seemed like a nice lady."

"I'm sure she is a nice lady," said Marie. "This is not what you think it is."

Taken for a Ride

The girls love roller coasters, but could Sage's little brother be the bravest of them all?

"Am I tall enough for this ride?" asked Noelle. She stood next to the sign with the bear holding his paw at 48 inches, the minimum height for riders on all of the scariest rides at Liberty Amusement Park.

"Not quite," joked Marie. "Maybe in ten or twenty years. You'd better stick with the baby boats."

Marie and her friends had volunteered to bring the younger Ivy Street kids to the park. Hailey chaperoned her younger sisters, Nicole and Emma. Sage had agreed to babysit her little brother, Joey. And Rose had asked to escort Caitlin, another of Hailey's sisters, around the park. Kenny, Noelle's little brother, preferred to wash the car with his dad, so Marie and Noelle were on their own.

They'd all arrived early and spread out through the park grounds, agreeing to meet at the Washington Pavilion at noon for lunch.

After a few hours of riding, Noelle and Marie climbed into The Flipper, strapped themselves in, and pulled down the bar. Over and over the girls tumbled as the ride went around and around, up and down. Now they were looking at the sky, now they were looking at the ground.

And when the ride stopped, and they finally tumbled off, Noelle said, "I think I . . . whoa!"

She caught hold of a lamppost to keep herself from falling. "I think I need to sit down."

"It's about noon," said Marie. "Let's go to the pavilion. It's so hot, and I could use a soda."

At the pavilion, Marie reached into the ice chest they'd brought. Everyone had been assigned to bring something for the picnic. Marie and Noelle had brought a dozen bottles of pop.

"Someone's beat us here," said Marie. She pointed to the ice chest. Ten bottles of pop stood there in the ice. Two bottles were missing.

Marie and Noelle each pulled out a bottle, twisted off the cap, and began to drink. The cold pop was just what they needed to cool off and settle their still-tumbling stomachs.

"I'm hungry," said Caitlin, who walked up holding a stuffed cat. "When can we eat?"

"I think it's too hot to eat," added Rose. "I'm just thirsty."

"Is it time for lunch yet?" It was Sage, with Joey. The boy reached up to hold his sister's hand.

"Hey, Sage," said Noelle. "Been on a lot of the rides today?"

"Oh, yeah," said Sage. "This kid just won't stop. He made me take him on The Colossus four times." The Colossus was the park's giant roller coaster, with corkscrews and steep plunges—the park's most popular attraction.

"And he didn't lose his lunch?" asked Noelle.

"Lunch!" said Joey. "I want lunch."

"Soon, Joey," said Sage. "Yeah, Joey loves the scary rides. I'm the one who can hardly stand them!"

"Lunch!" shouted Joey.

"I think it's close enough to noon to eat," said Marie. "Why don't we break out some sodas and sandwiches, and while we're eating, Sage can tell us what she and Joey were really doing."

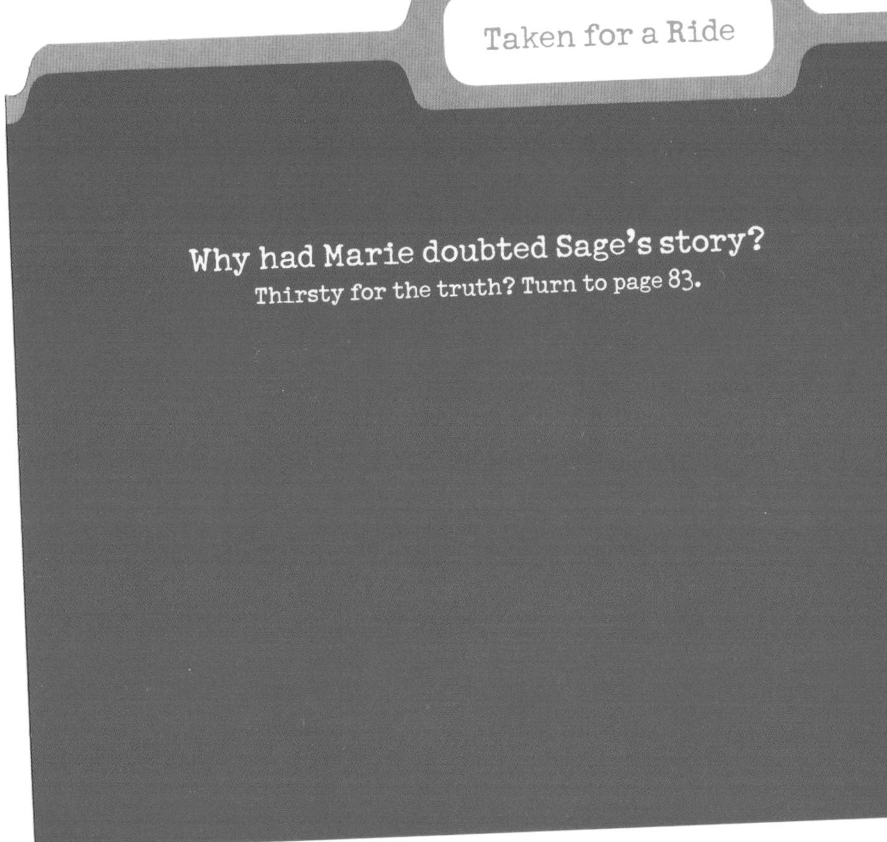

Looking for Catspurr

Can Marie's bravery put an end to a ghost story, Friday the 13th—and a whole lot of screaming?

"Sarah's asleep in her room," said Mrs. Ferris, Hailey's mom. "I'll leave the baby monitor on your dresser so that you can hear her if she wakes up. Have fun, girls. We'll be home around eleven."

Sarah was the Ferrises' baby daughter, just six months old.

"We won't be frightened, Mom," said Caitlin, Hailey's younger sister, with a wicked grin. "Even though it's Friday the 13th, when ghosts like to roam, and we'll be home alone, in the dark."

"Stop joking, Caitlin," said Mrs. Ferris. "You'll terrify Nicole and Emma." She hugged Hailey's two young sisters before scooting out the door with Mr. Ferris.

And then there was silence.

Suddenly Hailey wasn't sure she wanted to babysit. She'd babysat many times before, but she'd never babysat on Friday the 13th.

At least she had company. Noelle and Marie had come over to help her with her four younger sisters, particularly

Caitlin, who was a handful. Caitlin was obsessed with a particular ghost and claimed to be an expert about it.

"How would we know if there were a ghost?" Emma asked Caitlin. "Would we hear it?"

"There's no such thing as ghosts," said Hailey, hoping that she sounded convincing enough to her little sister. "Caitlin was just joking."

"It would just come up to you, shake your hand, and say, 'Hi, I'm a ghost. Who are you?'" Caitlin said.

"No," said Marie, leaning down to Emma. "It wouldn't say a word, because ghosts aren't real, and when's the last time you heard something that wasn't real speak?"

"Cartoons aren't real and they speak," added Nicole.

"But my ghost *is* real," Caitlin said. "It's a girl who cries because she misses her cat. His name is Catspurr, the Friendly Cat. The girl wanders this house weeping and wailing, hoping that she'll get her cat back."

"Stop teasing," said Hailey, picking up Snowball, Emma's cat, and rubbing her head.

"Let's get this party started," Marie said to Emma. "How about a game?"

"Ghosts in the Graveyard!" yelled Caitlin.

"No," said Hailey. "We'll play Monopoly, where the worst thing that happens is you land on Boardwalk with a hotel and lose all your money."

The rest of the girls agreed, and they began to play.

Two hours later, the game ended, and the girls climbed into their beds and drifted off to sleep. The last asleep was Snowball, cuddled in Emma's arms.

At eleven, a hand reached into the room, turned off the light, and closed the door. (Note: the hand belonged to Mrs. Ferris, who had said she'd be home at eleven.)

All was quiet—until the wailing began. The wails turned to screams, moans, and cries.

"Quiet," said Hailey, who wanted to go back to sleep.

"It's Snowball," said Nicole. "Emma, make your cat be quiet. She's waking up everyone."

"It's not Snowball," said Emma. "She's still asleep."

"It . . . it . . . it's the ghost!" whispered Caitlin, turning over. “It’s the same sound I hear every night. She just wants her cat.” With that said, Caitlin dozed back off to sleep.

“The ghost!” the younger girls screamed.

Hailey sat up. So did Marie and Noelle. That’s when they heard the singing, the soft singing.

“Another ghost!” shouted Emma.

“I can fix this,” said Marie. She jumped out of bed, and a moment later, the singing had stopped.

Looking for Catspurr

What had Marie done?

Haunted by the question? Turn to page 83.

Letters from an Admirer

Someone really likes Noelle. But is it the person she thinks it is?

"Did you get my cousin's letter?" Ben asked Noelle. "He said he was going to write you as soon as he got home."

"Did I ever," said Noelle. "So far he's sent five letters."

"What's this?" asked Marie. "You haven't told me this. Come on, spill it."

"It's nothing," said Noelle, blushing. "It's just . . .well . . . Ben introduced me to his cousin Joseph a little over a month ago when he was visiting. Joseph didn't talk to me much. But I keep getting letters from him. I just opened this one." She held up the letter.

"Let me read it," said Marie. She took the letter from Noelle's hand and read it to herself:

Dear Noelle,

Can't write much. Very busy. Just wanted to drop you a note from Williamsburg. You and my cousin Ben should come out sometime.

Well, gotta go. Tell my cousin I said "hi". I miss you. You know how much I like you.

Joseph

P.S. Did you get the locket I sent you? I saw it in a shop yesterday and knew you would like it.

Marie looked at the envelope. The letter had been sent from Williamsburg two days ago. "I'd love to visit the east coast, too," said Marie.

"Joseph's been sending me a letter every week," Noelle said. "He's so thoughtful."

"Wow," said Marie. "He must really like you."

"I'm jealous," said Ben. "He hasn't sent me any letters—or called since he left. So, did you get the locket? What does it look like? Do you like it?"

"I do," said Noelle. "It has a raccoon on the front, and a photo of a raccoon inside. How did he know I like raccoons?"

"How would he not?" said Ben. "You're always drawing raccoons on your notebooks."

"Yeah, maybe," said Noelle. "And I must have been wearing my raccoon T-shirt when we met."

Marie had a funny look on her face. She said, "The guy who sent you that locket, and the letters, must really like you. Maybe someday he'll be brave enough to tell you."

"But he has," said Noelle. "Joseph tells me he likes me in every one of his letters."

"No, I don't think he does," said Marie.

Letters from an Admirer

What did Marie mean?

For a letter-perfect answer, turn to page 83.

BOO!

Hailey discovers a message from a ghost. Should she decode its meaning, reply, or just go back to sleep?

You're not supposed to go to sleep early at a sleepover.

And you're not supposed to go to sleep at all after watching a scary movie.

But the girls had chased each other all day in sprinkler tag, water balloon fights, and sponge tag. And after a dinner of pizza and hot chocolate, somewhere about the time the ghost first appeared in the movie, the girls dropped off to sleep.

So by the time the haunted movie family found out who the ghost really was, all the girls were out. They lay like mummies in a tomb, wrapped in their blankets, lying on Brooke's bedroom floor, couch, and bed.

And then suddenly—a scream!

The lights flipped on.

Marie jumped up and looked around. The first thing she saw was herself, reflected in the window. The second thing she saw was the clock on the dresser showing 10:08. Just then it clicked over to 10:09. At 10:09, the night had barely begun! She turned to see who had screamed.

Noelle stood at the light switch. "It was Hailey who screamed!" shouted Noelle. "Look!"

Hailey was white as a ghost. And she was shivering.

"What's wrong, Hailey?" asked Brooke. "Did you have a nightmare?"

"N-n-n-no," said Hailey. "Well, yeah, I did. I was dreaming about ghosts haunting a family. Like in the movie. But then I woke up. And I saw the word 'BOO!' "

"Are you sure it wasn't just part of the dream?" asked Noelle. "You can wake up and still be dreaming."

"I was awake," said Hailey. "But I wasn't dreaming. I'm sure of it. I saw the word 'BOO!' right over there somewhere."

Hailey pointed at one of the walls. Marie followed her finger to a dresser covered in knickknacks, a few books, a lamp, and a digital clock. She also saw a window with open curtains and a painting of a cat.

"I'll bet it was that cat picture," said Noelle. "Look at those big eyes, like two big Os, as in 'BOO.' And cats' eyes glow in the dark."

"It wasn't the cat picture," said Hailey. "I saw the word 'BOO!' Besides, that's a painting of a cat. Painted eyes don't glow in the dark."

"They do if you use glow-in-the-dark paint," said Noelle. "It's the latest."

"My cat's eyes have never glowed before," said Brooke, who shivered and had turned white herself. "So I believe Hailey!"

"Then check the window," said Noelle. "Maybe someone was playing a joke."

"The window's closed," said Brooke. "And locked."

"Maybe someone held something in the window," said

Noelle. "You know those neighbor boys!"

"If it's a ghost," Brooke said, trying to act calmer, "I think we'd all better sleep in another room."

"Or another house," added Hailey.

"Or maybe we should all just go back to sleep here," said Marie. "There were no neighbor boys. And there was no ghost. And Hailey was awake. And she did see something. But it wasn't 'BOO!'"

BOO!

What had Hailey seen?

You'll find the answer on page 83 of this booooo—k.

Same Time, Same Place

If you do something and don't break a rule, how can you do the exact same thing and break it?

"We'll have to do this again," said Hailey as she slipped on her sandals.

"It was fun," said Marie.

Noelle nodded. "Only my house next time."

It hadn't been anything major, nothing particularly outstanding. It had just been a fun afternoon with friends—homemade pizza, charades, playing against the TV contestants on the girls' favorite show, *Guess Which Dog*, which came on every Saturday at 6:30 P.M. But just as the final credits rolled, and the sun began to set into the late summer horizon, it was time for Hailey to hurry home. Family rule: Home by sunset.

Hailey said good-bye, grabbed another slice of pizza, and raced out the door.

Then, a week before Halloween, Noelle decided it was time for another pizza party. "Remember our little party last August?" she asked Marie and Hailey.

"Party?" said Hailey.

"You remember—pizza, charades, *Guess Which Dog,* me, you, Marie?"

Hailey smiled. "Oh, yeah! That was so fun."

"How about this Saturday?" asked Noelle.

"I'm afraid I'm spending Friday night with my grandma," said Marie.

"Oh," said Noelle and Hailey together.

"But I'll be home by 3:00 on Saturday. We started at 4:00 before, so if we start at the same time, I can make it."

"Great!" said Noelle. "Be at my house at 4:00."

Hailey and Marie showed up at Noelle's doorstep at 4:00 on the dot. Marie was about to knock when Noelle opened the door and welcomed them in.

The girls tried to repeat their exact steps from the last party—after all, it had been so perfectly timed that the pizzas were ready just as their show began. First, they started the pizza. They mixed together the pizza dough ingredients—yeast, sugar, flour, salt, oil, and water.

Next, they played charades while the pizza dough rose.

Then, as soon as the dough had risen, they divided it into three pieces so that each could create her favorite pizza: cheese and mushroom for Hailey; ham and pineapple for Noelle; pepperoni for Marie.

And they cleaned up while the pizzas baked.

Finally, just as the theme song to their show began, the pizzas were ready.

The girls ate as they watched *Guess Which Dog.*

And when the final credits rolled, Hailey got up and pulled on her boots. “My house next time!” she said.

“Sure,” said Marie. “Oh, no! I’m sorry, Hailey. I should have known this would happen.” Marie hit her forehead with her palm and grabbed her jacket. “Noelle, you and I had better walk Hailey home. Then maybe she won’t get into trouble.”

Take your time before turning to page 83.

Witch Lady

Everyone expects to see witches on Halloween. But what happens if you think you see a real one?

It was Halloween, and it was just starting to get dark. Hope, Marie, and Noelle were taking Hope's little brother, Davy, up and down the neighborhood streets, trick-or-treating. The girls, of course, were too old to be scared by Halloween horrors, but they had fun seeing Davy's delighted reaction to the ghosts, ghouls, and monsters.

And then they turned the corner and saw the mansion.

"Who lives here?" asked Hope.

Odd. They had no idea who lived here. And they'd visited this neighboring street many times.

"Trick-or-treat?" said Davy, pointing toward the house.

Maybe they hadn't noticed the old mansion because of the tall wrought-iron gate. It did send "Keep Out" vibes.

Or maybe the dark, overgrown ivy had hidden the house from easy view.

Or maybe they always had been too busy chatting and simply had never noticed the place before.

But now they noticed—the turrets, the black shutters, the wild garden, the scarecrows, the menacing jack-o'-lanterns, and the things hiding in the shadows.

Suddenly, a swishing shadow walked toward them. "It's Wanda's house!" the shadow shouted.

The startled girls peered down. A miniature pirate had appeared from nowhere. He wore a patch over his eye and held a paper box shaped like a treasure chest.

"Wanda? Who's Wanda?" Marie asked the boy.

"Wanda. You know, Wanda," said the pirate. "She's the witch lady." A shiver ran up the girls' spines.

"A . . . a . . . a witch lady?" asked Hope. "And you like her?"

"Yeah," said the boy. "She's nice and intewesting."

"Is she scary?" asked Marie.

"No," said the boy. "And she has a kitty."

"A black kitty?" asked Noelle, mentally taking notes.

"How did you know?" said the boy. "The kitty's name is Wail. He's a skinny cat."

"I like kitties, too," said Davy. He tugged on his sister's hand, trying to pull her toward the house, but she didn't budge.

The girls peered into the yard. Was that a flash of black they saw in the shadows?

"And she has a puppy named Wayne," said the boy. "He wets on things."

"I like puppies, too," said Davy. He tugged harder on Noelle's hand.

"Wayne?" said Hope. "What kind of dog name is that?"

"And what does it have to do with wetting on things?" asked Noelle. "This is getting weirder and weirder."

"You should go see Wanda," said the boy. "She gave me a big bag of candy."

"Bag of candy! Bag of candy!" said Davy. This time the boy tried to let go of Noelle, but just as he thought he could make his escape, his sister grabbed him by his dragon tail.

"She's just trying to fatten you up," said Hope.

"I think we should trick-or-treat her," said Marie.

"Are you crazy?" said Noelle. "I don't want to trick-or-treat a witch. She'll probably turn me into a frog."

"Yeah," added Hope, "or a bat."

"I like bats," said Davy.

"Oh, I don't think you need to worry," said Marie. She slipped Davy's hand into hers, pushed open the gate, and headed toward the house.

Witch Lady

Why wasn't Marie worried about the "witch lady"?

If your mind's playing tricks on you, turn to page 85.

Cousin Sam

Jealousy, vanity, frustration—how can a cousin's visit cause such an uproar?

"My cousin Sam is going to be here for Thanksgiving," Rose told Marie and Noelle when she ran into them on the school playground.

"Sam the Star?" asked Noelle excitedly. "Cool!"

"I don't know if Sam's a star," said Rose. "It was only a walk-on role in a made-for-TV movie."

"Yeah, but still, millions of people saw that movie," said Noelle. "Sam will be famous someday."

"I think so," said Rose, "but I am biased. Anyway, we want to have a party the day after Thanksgiving, with maybe you two, me, some boys from class. Eat leftovers, play some games, talk."

"I'm in," said Noelle.

"I'll be there," said Marie.

"Where will you be?" asked Hope, who had walked up.

"Party at Rose's house," said Noelle, "for Rose's cousin, Sam. It'll be on Friday, the day after Thanksgiving."

"I'm there," said Hope. "I bunked with Sam at French camp two years ago."

"Maybe we can audition for movie roles," joked Noelle.

Rose laughed. "You wish. Maybe a romantic comedy starring you and Ben."

"Somebody talking about me?" It was Ben, accompanied by Matt and Nate.

"Yeah," said Noelle. "Rose's cousin Sam is going to make us movie stars. We're all invited to Rose's house for a party and auditions."

"Hey, there'll be enough ham at the party without you guys acting out, too," said Rose. "This is strictly for fun."

"What's for fun?" asked Nate.

"Rose's party," said Ben. "My brother wants to be an actor. He should come to the party, too."

"What party?" asked Matt.

"Listen closely," said Rose. "I'm going to say this once.

My cousin Sam—"

"—the movie star," said Noelle.

"—the made-for-TV-movie walker-on," Rose continued, "is going to be in town for Thanksgiving. We're throwing a party on Friday. You're invited. We'll play—"

"—charades, so that Sam can see how fine an actor I am," Noelle interrupted again.

"Right," grumbled Ben. Suddenly he wasn't so sure if he wanted to go to this party. "We get it. You love Sam."

"We'll play non-acting games to drive Noelle nuts," said Rose.

Hope piped up. "Sage and I will re-enact our heart-wrenching roles as the stars of our school play, *The Pet Shop*. Let's invite the whole cast. We can do the play again. Sam will love it!"

"Anyway," said Rose, "Sam had a lot of fun last summer and wants to hang out with all you guys."

"Who's Sam?" asked Matt.

"Sam! My cousin!" said Rose. "Maybe Sam and I will

just go to a movie."

"Sam's O.K.," Ben said to Matt, "but he's not that amazing. I should know. I spent a lot of time with him last summer."

"No, you *don't* know," said Marie.

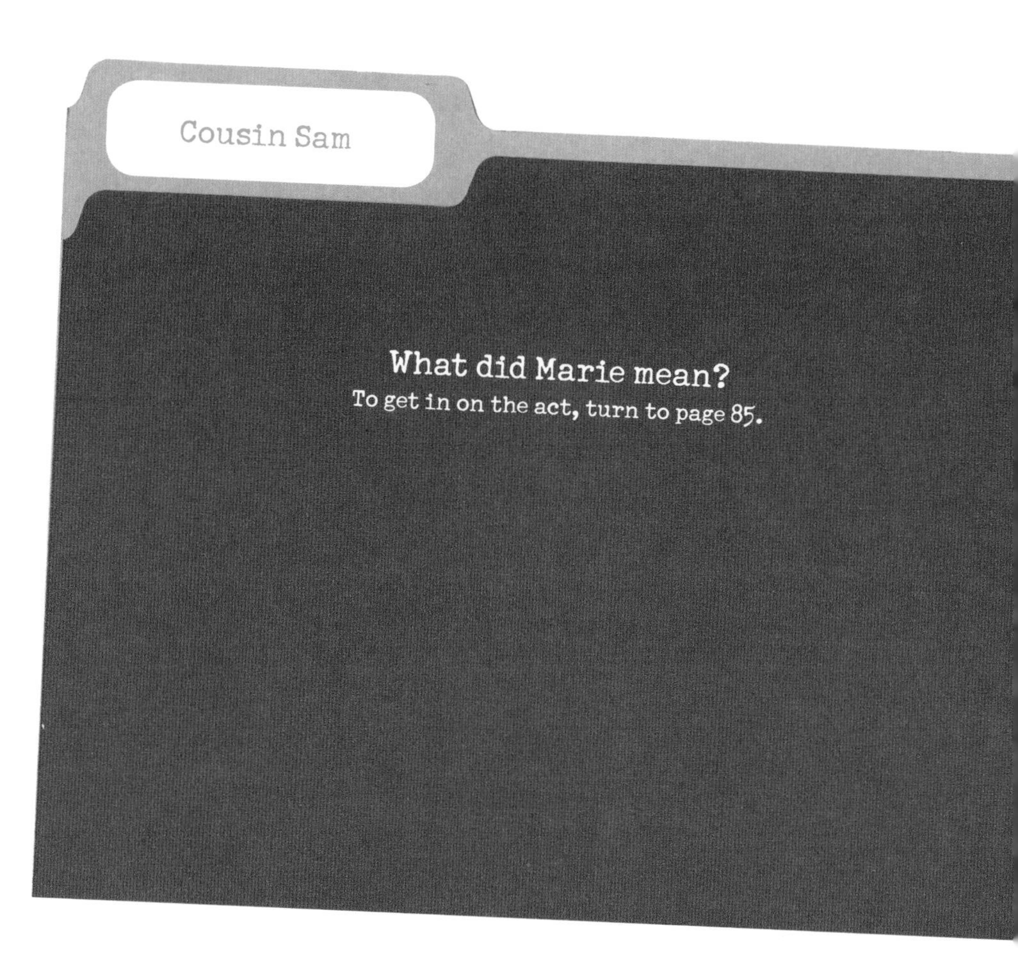

The Well-Wishers

Hailey has the flu. Now her friends hope to be the first ones to wish her well—will they succeed?

"So, what do you have?" asked Noelle. "Measles? Mumps? Malaria?"

"Just the flu," said Hailey. The girls took a step back. They liked Hailey, but they'd rather not catch what she had. "I came down with it yesterday. Mom says I should be O.K. in a day or two."

Noelle, Marie, Brooke, and Faith were visiting their sick friend. They'd brought homemade cookies and get-well balloons with them.

"Where should we put these, boss?" asked Brooke, who held the floating balloons.

"Tie them there." Hailey pointed to the foot of her bed. "That way I can see them." Brooke tied the balloons to the rail on the bed.

"When you're feeling bored, throw balls of socks at the balloons and try to hit them," said Noelle.

"You're going to love these cookies!" Faith carried the plate over to Hailey and slipped it under her nose.

"I can't smell them, but they look good," said Hailey. "Maybe later, if I can taste anything."

"We could help you out," said Brooke, "since you're suffering so." She reached for a couple of cookies.

"Save some for Hailey's sisters," said Faith. Then she took a handful of cookies, too.

"Are we your first well-wishers?" asked Noelle.

Hailey pointed to her dresser. On it were rows and rows of get-well cards.

Marie picked one up and looked at it. "Pretty." She read the inside message. "From Louise! Who's Louise?"

"She's my aunt in Minnesota. She's a riot. You need to meet her next time she visits."

"Here's one from an Uncle Bob, and one from a grandma, and one from an Aunt Wendy. You sure do have a lot of relatives."

"All over the country," said Hailey. "And one uncle lives in Brazil. His card is that green and yellow one."

"They must love you a lot to send all these cards when you're sick," said Noelle.

"We're close," said Hailey. "Even if we live far apart."

"It's nice to have close relatives," said Brooke.

"It's also nice to have close friends," said Hailey, "who bring me cookies and balloons."

"And who are the first ones to give you get-well wishes for this flu," said Marie.

"We're not the first," said Faith. "Look at all these get-well cards."

"Oh, we're the first, all right," said Marie. "Isn't that right, Hailey?"

Hailey smiled and nodded.

The Well-Wishers

How did Marie know?

Sick of guessing? Turn to page 85.

Cinderelephant

An actor's late for a play. Was it really an accident or accidentally on purpose?

"Where's Sage?" asked Hope. "The play starts in just five minutes."

"I saw her this afternoon," said Noelle. "She said she'd be here."

To combat post-holiday winter doldrums, the kids had convinced their school to let them put on a play. Noelle and Brooke had written the play, *Cinderelephant.* Hope was the director, and most of their friends were in it.

"Sage doesn't have to go onstage until the second act," said Noelle. "Maybe she'll show up by then."

"I hope so," said Hope, who was a little nervous. She'd been in many plays before, but this was the first time she'd directed one. "If not, what will I do?"

"Her role's not that important," said Brooke, adjusting her large head as she walked up. "So even if she doesn't make it, we'll be just fine."

And then, it was showtime.

The curtain rose on Noelle, Cinderelephant, scrubbing her floor at the zoo.

Enter the wicked step-rhinos—Rose and Brooke. The audience laughed at the silly costumes the girls wore.

The first half of the play was filled with songs, dances, and elephant jokes.

Then it was intermission.

"Sage still isn't here!" said Hope. "What are we going to do? The ballroom scene's coming up next!"

"Go on without her," said Noelle.

"But Russell will look silly dancing by himself!"

"If all you need is a dancer, I can help," said Hailey. She went out into the audience, grabbed her sister Caitlin, and led her backstage. "Here, put Caitlin in Sage's costume."

"Cool!" shouted Caitlin. "I get to star in a middle school play. Wait till I tell my friends."

"I wouldn't exactly say 'star,'" said Hailey.

But in a couple of minutes, Caitlin was ready, looking appropriately hideous in her hippo costume. Hailey and Russell showed her what to do, and the second half of the play began.

Caitlin did just fine. No one knew that she was a last-minute substitution, even though she was just a dancer at Prince Pachyderm's ball.

After the play ended, the audience clapped and cheered. The performers, writers, and director all took their bows. And the curtain closed.

"Sorry I'm late," said Sage, suddenly rushing onto the stage. "Is it over? I'm so sorry! I ran all the way here. My parents were late getting back from shopping, and I couldn't leave Joey alone." Joey was her little brother.

"It's O.K.," said Hope. "Caitlin filled in for you."

"Sorry again," said Sage. "At least I can help clean up."

In no time, everything was in order and the girls all headed home together. A full moon shining on the snow-covered ground lit their path. Marie and Sage led the way.

"Look," said Sage. "I'm walking back home in the same footprints I made coming here."

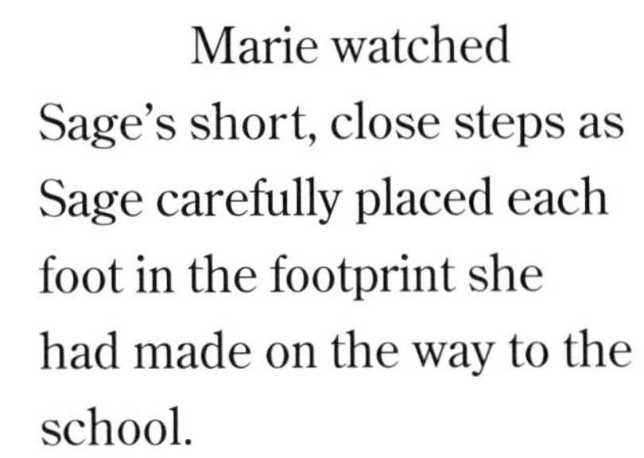

Marie watched Sage's short, close steps as Sage carefully placed each foot in the footprint she had made on the way to the school.

Sage continued walking in her footprints until the group reached her house. "Next time we do a play, I'll ask my parents not to be late."

The girls said good night and then continued on their way—all except for Marie. "You guys go on," she said. "I need to ask Sage something."

After their friends left, Marie turned to Sage. "Why didn't you want to be in the play?"

"What do you mean, Marie? I did all I could to get to the school on time. It wasn't my fault that I had to babysit."

"Oh, I think you had plenty of time to make it," said Marie. "And you can tell me the truth, you know."

"A minor role, an ugly costume, and I had to dance with Russell," Sage blurted out. "I feel awful, but I didn't want to hurt Hope's feelings. Anyway, how did you know?"

How did Marie know?

Played out? Turn to page 85.

The Skeleton's Hand

A skeleton steals Marie's diary to seek revenge. Or does Hailey have something up her sleeve?

It happened during the cold of early winter. The trees were bare, and a sharp wind shrieked and moaned. But inside the cabin the girls were warm. They were spending the week at Hailey's uncle's cabin. They'd done some skiing, some sledding, some skating.

And then a snowstorm drove them inside. Hailey's parents left for a dinner party two cabins over, so Noelle took advantage of the time to read a book she had brought. Hope and Sage played card games. Marie got caught up in her diary. Hailey baked cookies.

In the evening, as the windows darkened and the storm howled, Hailey had a suggestion. "Let's tell spooky stories!"

Everyone thought it was a great idea. Marie set her diary on the end table next to her chair. Hope and Sage put away their cards. Noelle shelved her book. And Hailey brought out a plate of cookies and set it on Marie's end table.

The stories began.

Marie told the story of "The Itchy Ghost."

Noelle told "The Headless Dog."

Then Hailey began the story of "The Skeleton's Hand."

"Bones. Long, long bones. That's all it was," she began. "And it was proud of those bones. They glowed white in the night, and they rattled and clanked as it walked. The skeleton scared everyone—animal and human—who saw it. It loved to scare the townspeople around here.

"But, finally, the locals had had enough. They lit torches, and they tracked that skeleton down. 'No more will you frighten our children!' they shouted. And one local swung his shovel at the skeleton.

"The skeleton held up a hand to defend itself, but the shovel knocked the hand into the bushes.

"The skeleton knew it was outnumbered. It didn't want to lose any more bones. So it turned and ran off into the night and was never seen again.

"And the townspeople thought that was the end.

"But it wasn't. For the skeleton's hand crawled out of the bushes and went to seek revenge. From house to house it crawled, taking and taking. The people had taken away a prized possession—its body. So it took prized possessions away from them—wedding rings, baby pictures, letters from loved ones, special gifts, and favorite toys. No one knew where these things had gone. They only knew that important parts of their lives were suddenly missing.

"The taking continues today. Even though all the original townspeople are long gone, the skeleton's hand still takes revenge on anyone who hears this story." Hailey looked around the room at her friends. They were hugging pillows or pulling up their feet from the floor to their seats. So she added, ". . . and that means you. Keep a close eye out when you sleep tonight!"

“O.K., Hailey,” said Noelle, “what did the skeleton’s hand take from you?”

“My baby teeth. And because of that, I didn’t get any money from the tooth fairy.” Noelle threw a pillow at Hailey.

Hailey caught the pillow and asked, “More cookies, anyone?” Everyone nodded, so she slipped her hand under the empty cookie plate, lifted it from the end table with both hands, and hurried into the kitchen.

As soon as Hailey was back, Hope said, “My turn.”

She told the story of “The Mummy Mommy.”

Sage told “The Wolves at the Cabin Door.”

“Then the wolf slowly turned the handle—”

Suddenly, a loud scratching sound came from the window, and all the girls screamed and jumped. They laughed when they discovered that it was just the wind blowing a branch against the window.

“Well, so much for going to bed after that,” said Noelle. “I’m going to keep reading and try to forget about mummies and wolves and skeleton hands.”

The rest of the girls were also too spooked to sleep. Hailey joined Hope and Sage in a card game. Marie turned to go back to writing in her diary—

“My diary’s gone!” Marie shouted.

“It’s the skeleton’s hand!” Noelle said quickly. “You heard the story, and now it’s taken your prized possession.”

“Then maybe that wasn’t just the wind after all,” added Sage. “Maybe it was the skeleton’s hand looking for ways in.

I wonder if it got in through the back door?"

Hope shivered. "Who's next?" she whispered.

"Oh, I wouldn't worry," said Marie. "I know who took my diary, and I think I know where it is."

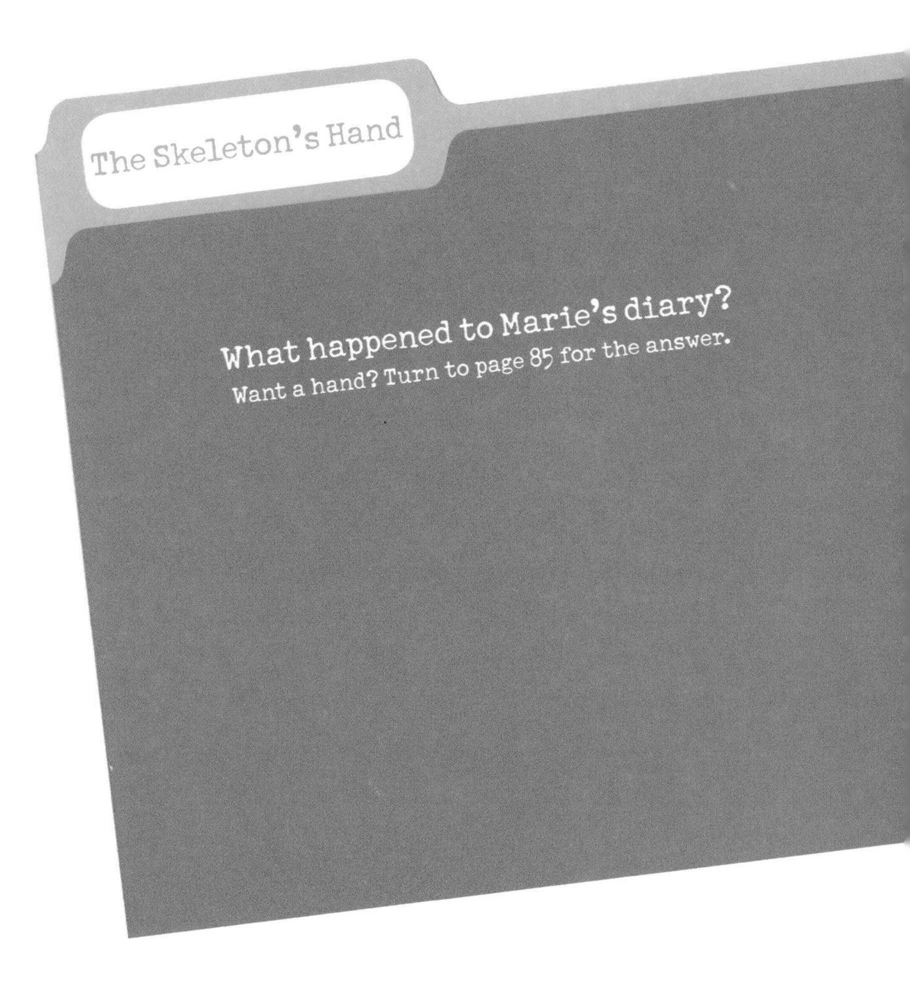

Goody, Goody, Guava Drops

Four guys. Four valentine treats. Will the girls be able to figure out Hailey's admirers?

"I got twenty-two candy hearts from class valentines and six candy bars from my grandparents," said Brooke. "So, what did you get?"

Noelle looked at her collection. "Twenty-three candy hearts and some heart-shaped cookies that my mom made."

"Bag of chocolate kisses," said Marie.

"I got Rice Krispie treats, a chocolate heart, a candy bar from England, and Guava Drops," said Hailey.

The girls had gotten together at Hailey's house for their own day-after-Valentine's party to read each other's valentines and to snack on sweets. Valentines and treats covered the kitchen table.

"What are Guava Drops?" asked Brooke, holding up the bag of colorful candy.

"They're a gummy candy made from guava," said Hailey, reaching for the bag to read the ingredients. "It's a fruit."

"Sounds disgusting," said Brooke, slipping a chocolate into her mouth. "Who gave them to you, your dad?"

Hailey's dad was in the international export business and was always traveling to foreign lands and bringing back unusual gifts for his wife and daughters.

"It's a secret," said Hailey. She smiled mysteriously.

"Aha!" said Noelle. "So it was a boy."

"Maybe."

"O.K., tell us," said Marie.

"Guess!"

"Nate," said Brooke. Hailey liked Nate and had given him a chocolate heart last year.

"He gave me something nice, yes," said Hailey.

"Guava Drops?" asked Noelle.

"I didn't say that," said Hailey.

The girls named a few more boys. Hailey said, "No, no, no, no, no."

"Felipe?" guessed Noelle.

"I didn't say either way, and yes, Eric gave me something, too." Eric had come from England to live for a year with his aunt and uncle.

"So," said Marie. "Let's get this straight. You have four gifts and three givers so far. Who's the fourth?"

"Brooke already guessed," said Hailey.

"Your dad," said Brooke. "He gave you the Guava Drops. I knew it."

"He's the fourth, but I didn't say the Guava Drops came from him."

"O.K.," said Noelle. "So who would give you something so disgusting?"

"I'll give you a clue," said Hailey. "One of them gave me the same thing I gave him last year in class."

"That narrows it down a bit," said Noelle. "Give us

another clue."

"One brought me a chocolate bar. He bought the candy in England."

"It's obvious who that is," said Brooke. "One more clue should do it."

"Uh, one of them gave me something that has his name mixed up in it."

"Now I'm confused," said Brooke.

"I got it," said Marie. "Now I know who gave you the Guava Drops."

Goody, Goody, Guava Drops

Who gave Hailey the Guava Drops?

Wouldn't it be sweet to know? Turn to page 85.

It Walks at Midnight

Bigfoot roams the park. Or is it Stiff Foot?

Noelle's brother Patrick woke Noelle up to tell her the news. He'd gone out early that winter morning on a walk through the park, when he'd seen it—Bigfoot, Sasquatch, whatever it was. At least he'd seen its giant footprints.

"I followed them for a ways," Patrick said, "but I stopped because I didn't *really* want to meet it."

Noelle was thrilled. Part of her wanted to find the famous monster, get to know it, become friends with it, and understand what made it hide from people.

The smarter part of her wanted to stay far, far away, because who knows what a monster like that would do to you if it caught you.

The first part of her won.

She dressed quickly and ran next door to Marie's house. Marie was still asleep, so Noelle woke her up.

"Patrick's made a great discovery! Come on, Marie, we've gotta check this out. We're smart. We'll look at the clues and figure out how to find it."

"I don't think I want to find a giant," said Marie. "I like my arms attached to my body."

"Who has it ever hurt?" asked Noelle. "Please, for me? It's probably just a kind, shy, bunny-rabbit type who only wants a friend."

"I very much doubt that," said Marie. "But I'll go with you to the park, at least."

Marie dressed, and then the two girls raced out of the house and off to the park.

Apparently the news hadn't gotten around yet. No one else was there. The girls quickly found the set of huge footprints.

They were indeed large—about twenty inches long and ten inches wide. Each print had a big toe on the right side of the foot, with three more little toes. Only four toes! The footprints flattened the snow smooth.

In the middle were smaller footprints, probably Patrick's, from when he'd tracked the beast.

The girls followed the huge footprints across the park. Was it the cold of the morning or the thought of meeting a monster that sent shivers up Noelle's spine?

"CAW-CAW-CAW."

"What's that?" shouted Noelle. She grabbed on to Marie's coat.

"It's just a crow," whispered Marie.

They followed more prints past picnic tables, around a pavilion, between silent trees. And then, CRACK!

Noelle jumped.

A tree branch, heavy with snow, fell behind them.

The girls continued to follow the prints. Once they reached the main road, the prints disappeared on the cleanly plowed pavement.

Noelle looked around to see if the footprints resumed across the street, but she couldn't find any more.

"It's got to be behind us! Let's backtrack," said Noelle. "Maybe we can find where the tracks started from."

Suddenly, an eerie howl came from behind them. "Arrrooooo!" Noelle couldn't decide if it was a howl or a moan.

"Never mind," Noelle said as she grabbed Marie's arm.

"Let's get out of here!"

Marie smiled. "Fine with me," she said, "but I already know what's out there and where these prints came from."

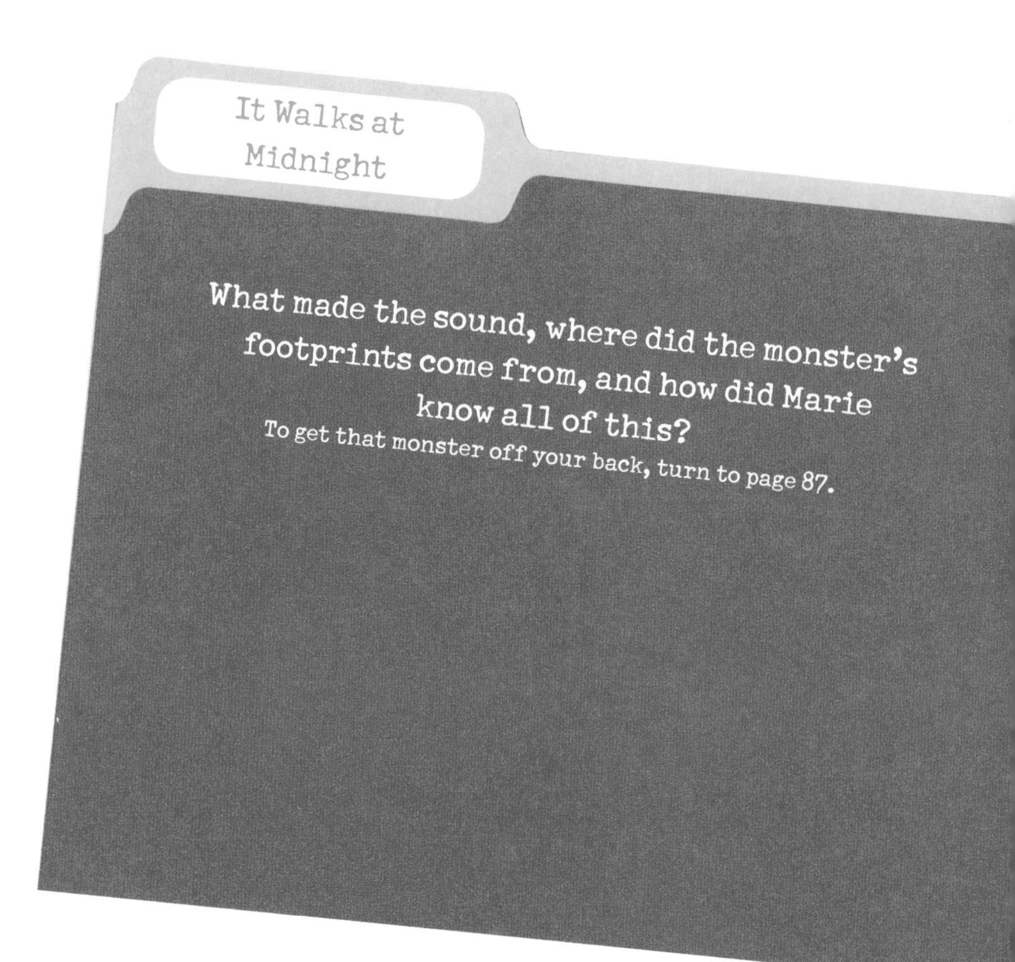

Cakewalk

Helping out at a carnival can be a lot of work.
But what if it's on your birthday?

Hailey, Brooke, Hope, Sage, Faith, Rose, Noelle, and Marie couldn't wait. The dazzling display of cakes that filled the large cafeteria table amazed them—not only did the table include their favorite cakes, but there were cakes the girls hadn't even known were their favorites!

"I'm going to win the bunny cake," said Faith.

"I'd go for the chocolate-chocolate-chocolate one," said Noelle. "It looks three times as delicious!"

Most of the carnival was held outside, circling the school playground, but the cakewalk and the food concessions were inside the gym/cafeteria. Slices of pizza and boxes of doughnuts covered the tables in half of the large room. The other half of the room was dedicated to the most popular event at the carnival—the cakewalk. In front of the stage, large paper numbers, carefully taped to the floor, formed a circle. Someone had tied back the stage curtains to reveal a CD player, a microphone, and a basket resting on a table. The basket brimmed with the ring numbers written out on slips of paper.

"By the time we're done helping out," said Hailey, "there won't be much to choose from." She stood in front of the table ogling the sweet cupcakes.

All the girls had volunteered to help out at different carnival booths. They'd signed up to work the first half so that they'd have the rest of the carnival free to hang out together.

"What about you, Marie?" said Noelle. "It's your birthday. Which cake would you want to win?"

Marie studied the cake table. "The vanilla hamster cake."

"You'd eat Chuckee?" asked Noelle. Chuckee was their classroom hamster.

"I think it's a cute cake," said Marie. "So, yes, I would eat Chuckee, if he were a cake."

"Some way to spend your birthday," said Rose, "working at a carnival."

"Having fun and hanging out with friends," said Marie. "I'll take it. Besides, this year is a family party year. My parents are taking me out to dinner on Saturday. Next year I'll have a friends party."

"Attention!" An announcement came from a woman at the microphone. "The first cakewalk starts in two minutes."

"Let's hit the booths, Marie," said Marie's mom. "You don't want to be late." Marie looked at her watch.

"You're right. I'm off, girls," said Marie. "Coming?"

"We'll be there soon," said Noelle. "I need to call my mom and tell her to come get me after the carnival's over."

Each of the girls mumbled something, so Marie rushed off with her mom, leaving her friends by the cake table.

Once she arrived at the fishpond booth, Marie stood up and peeked from behind the curtain to see who was next in line to fish. Her line seemed to be the longest at the carnival!

"Hi, Marie," said Noelle's mom as she walked by. "That's quite a line!"

"I know!" Marie said. "I hope these kids can fish fast!" Marie smiled and glanced around at the other booths.

Finally, Noelle had made it to her booth. She was helping Marie's mom in the ringtoss. And Marie's other friends were finally arriving at their booths. *They sure took their time getting to work!* Marie thought.

After an hour, Noelle walked over to the fishpond booth. "Come on, Marie. Our shift's up. Let's go see if there are any cakes left worth winning." The other girls walked over, too, so Marie handed her pole to the supervising mom.

"It looks like you leaned against the cake table, Noelle. There's vanilla frosting on your wrist."

"Yum!" said Noelle, licking it off.

The girls hurried into the gym. A cakewalk was in progress, but for some reason, the stage curtain was now closed, and everything was in front of the stage. The girls raced over to the cake table. The only desserts left were two plain cakes.

"Cake is cake," said Marie. "Let's win one and share it."

The girls each picked a place on the circle. The music began, and they walked. Then, silence.

Marie rushed to the nearest number—13. This didn't look good.

The supervising mom pulled a number from the basket. "You're the winner!" she said, smiling at Marie.

"Thirteen?" asked Marie, moving her foot to be sure.

"That's the number! Lucky 13." The mom quickly returned the number to the bowl. "Pick a cake," she said.

Marie looked over the two remaining cakes on the table. *Neither of them is as good as the hamster cake,* she thought. "I think—"

"—I think a birthday girl should get the cake she wants," said Noelle. And then she shouted, "Happy birthday!"

Suddenly, the stage curtain opened. There stood Marie's mom and dad holding a cake—the hamster cake.

Marie was stunned. She smiled as friends and family—and lots of strangers—sang "Happy Birthday."

Her friends all gave her a big group hug.

"Thank you, thank you, thank you," said Marie. "I didn't have a clue."

"Finally," said Noelle, "we surprised Marie."

Cakewalk

They had. But the clues were there for Marie. Did you see them?

Surprised yourself? Turn to page 87 to see why.

Absent Present

A Stormy Shortcut

The Long, Dark Hall

Poor Little Puppy

Give Me a Ring

Nobody's Home

The Neighbor's Garden

Taken for a Ride

Looking for Catspurr

Letters from an Admirer

Same Time, Same Place

Cousin Sam

The Well-Wishers

Cinderelephant

The Skeleton's Hand

Goody, Goody, Guava Drops

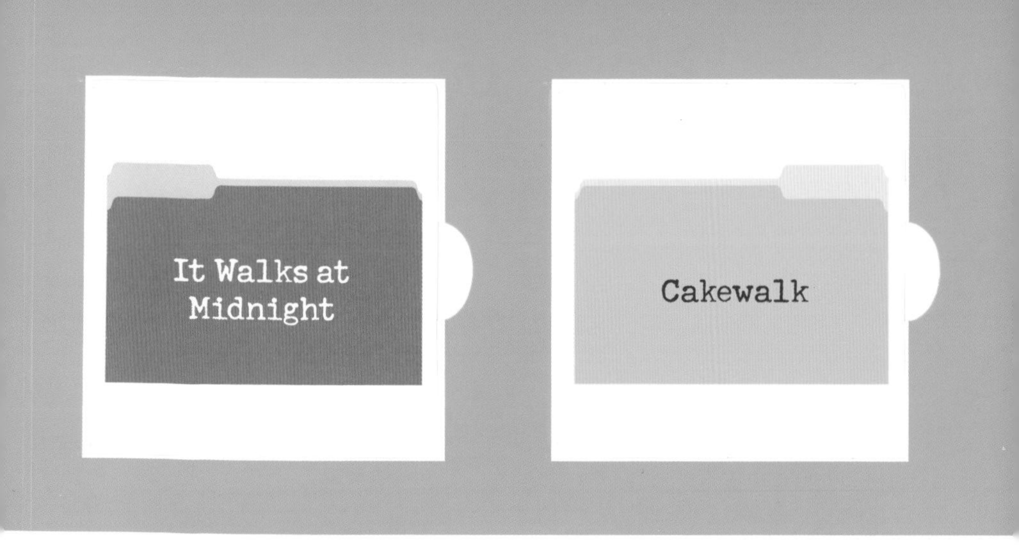

Did you like these mysteries?
Would you like some more?
Let us know!

Send your comments to:

Mini Mysteries Editor
American Girl
8400 Fairway Place
Middleton, WI 53562